£2.75

A BAD DREAM

1. One evening, Mr Lazy was in bed reading his favourite bedtime book called, 'Sleepytime Tales'.

2. But Mr Lazy was so lazy that he read only one page, then he yawned and fell sound asleep.

3. Suddenly, there came a loud knock at the door. Mr Lazy got up and went downstairs to open it.

4. It was little Miss Bossy. 'WAKE UP, WAKE UP!' she said. 'There's lots of WORK to be done!'

5. Mr Lazy groaned as little Miss Bossy marched him into the kitchen. 'First, the WASHING UP!' she said.

6. After that, she ordered Mr Lazy to wash his socks, dust all the furniture and polish the floor.

7. And so it went on . . . until the next morning, when Mr Lazy woke up! It had all been a terrible dream.

8. 'Phew!' sighed Mr Lazy. 'That dream *was* hard work!' Then do you know what? He went back to sleep!

MR. NOSEY'S NEW JOB

Mr Nosey was a nosey man. He was the sort of person who couldn't resist poking his nose into other people's business.

Which was annoying.

For instance. If you happened to be reading a book, Mr Nosey was the sort of person who would creep up behind you and peep over your shoulder to see what you were reading.

Or, if you happened to be talking to a friend and Mr Nosey was about, you may be sure he would listen to every word you said.

Every word!

That's how nosey he was.

Well, one day Mr Nosey decided to get a job. So he walked into Tiddletown, which is where he lived, and bought a newspaper.

The first job he saw advertised was for a window cleaner.

'Hm!' thought Mr Nosey. 'That looks interesting.'

And he got the job.

But Mr Nosey just couldn't resist peeping through people's windows while he was cleaning them, to see what was going on inside.

The Tiddletown folk didn't like that one little bit.

And they told him so.

Which is why Mr Nosey didn't last long in that job.

6

Mr Nosey read the advertisements again, and the very next day, he got a job at the Tiddletown telephone exchange.

'Number please?' asked Mr Nosey the telephone operator. 'Hold on, I'll put you through.'

But the trouble was, Mr Nosey couldn't resist holding on, too.

He listened to all the other people's telephone conversations! In fact, he spent all day just listening to the Tiddletown gossip!

Well, people didn't like that at all and they complained to the telephone manager.

So, Mr Nosey didn't last long in that job.

Then one afternoon, Mr Nosey found a job that suited him down to the ground. Or rather, it suited him down to the end of his nose.

It was the very job for a man like Mr Nosey, who loved peeking and prying into other people's affairs.

Can you guess what it was?

I'll tell you.

He got a job as a detective at the Tiddletown police station!

'There's a spot of trouble down at the bakery,' said the police sergeant to Mr Nosey, one day. 'Just go down there and find out what's going on, please.'

'Certainly,' smiled Mr Nosey.

And he did. He was very good at it. Very good indeed.

Then, only the other morning, Mr Herd, the farmer, lost one of his pigs. So he telephoned the sergeant at the police station.

'Could you send someone down to the farm to help me find my missing pig?' he asked.

'Certainly!' said the sergeant. 'We've got just the man for the job!'

I'll bet you can guess who that was, can't you?

That's right.

Mr Nosey, the detective!

Mr Nosey set off straightaway. The first thing he came to was a barn.

'I wonder if Mr Herd's pig is in there?' he thought to himself, creeping quietly inside.

But the pig wasn't there.

Then, Mr Nosey thought he heard a noise coming from behind a fence. So he crept quietly up to the fence and peeped over the top.

But the pig wasn't there.

In fact, Mr Nosey spent all day looking for the pig. He went peeking and prying all over the farm. Peeping over hedges and looking behind trees until . . . he found the pig, fast asleep, under some straw.

In the pig sty!

Mr Herd *was* pleased.

'How did you find it?' he asked.

Mr Nosey smiled, modestly.

It was easy,' he said. 'I just followed my NOSE!'

MR. HAPPY ON HOLIDAY

1. One year, Mr Happy sat at home trying to think where to spend his summer holiday. He looked through all the travel books. But could he make up his mind where to go? He could not!

2. Then one afternoon, the telephone rang. It was Mr Uppity. 'Come to my new luxury Holiday Camp,' he said. 'Its got three swimming pools, six tennis courts and a fun fair!'

3. Mr Happy smiled. 'It sounds just the place for me,' he said.
So Mr Happy packed his suitcase and walked to the railway
station and caught a train all the way to the Holiday Camp.

4. When Mr Happy arrived, Mr Uppity showed him to his bedroom.
'Mr Noisy is in the room next to yours,' explained Mr Uppity.
'But don't worry,' he smiled. 'His room is SOUNDproofed!'

5. The next day, Mr Happy went for a swim. He found Mr Busy busily trying out all three swimming pools at once. 'Hello,' said Mr Busy. SPLASH. 'Goodbye!' SPLASH. 'Can't stop!' SPLASH.

6. Then Mr Happy met little Miss Scatterbrain. She was carrying a cricket bat. 'Care for a game?' she invited. 'Cricket?' asked Mr Happy. 'No, not cricket,' she replied. 'Tennis!'

7. Mr Happy spent two weeks at Mr Uppity's holiday camp. He had a wonderful time there and met nearly all his friends. Nearly all. One friend was rather late. Can you guess who?

8. It was little Miss Late. She was late, as usual. In fact, she didn't arrive for her summer holiday at the Holiday Camp until mid-December. Can you believe it? Six months late!

DOTTY PUZZLES

What are these Mr Men looking at? Join the dots to find out.

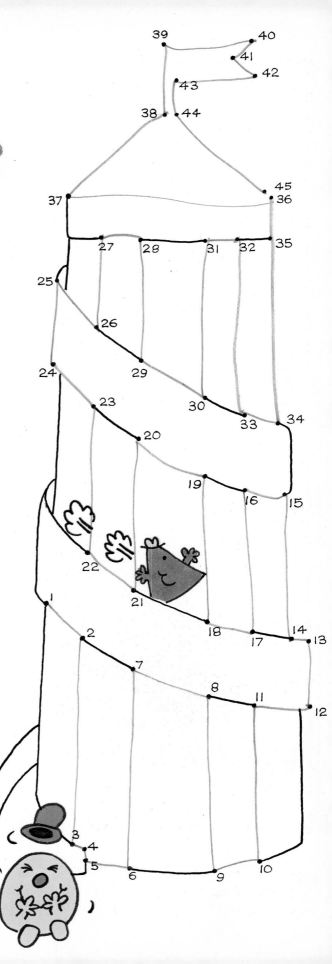

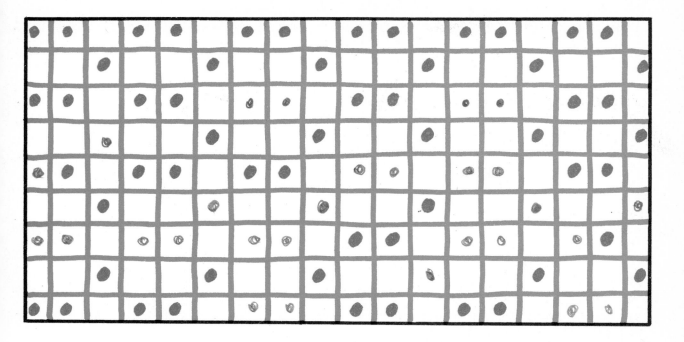

Little Miss Dotty has lost some of the dots from her dotty wallpaper. Can you put back the missing dots so that the pattern is continued?

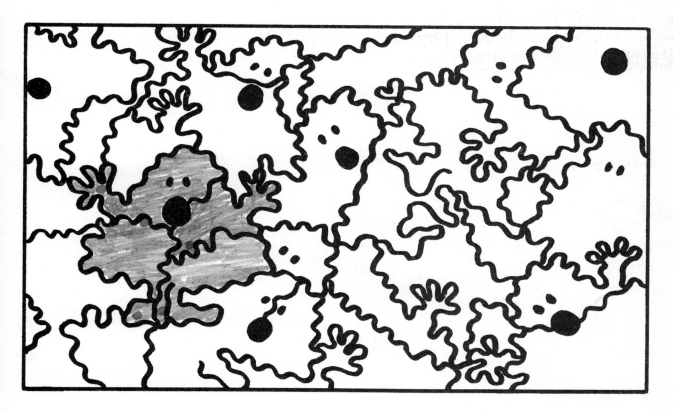

Mr Jelly is frightened of everything and anything. He is hiding from something or someone in the picture. Colour in all the parts marked with a pink dot to make him reappear.

These Mr Men and Little Miss look a little different from usual. Can you find ten differences?

Mr Fussy likes everything to be neat and in its proper place. Tidy this page for him by matching the right pieces together to make three squares.

Answer: A and D; B and F; C and E.

Good morning, Mr. Topsy-Turvy!

Morning good.

Why can you never get anything the round way right?

Catching isn't it!

19

little Miss Fickle's DIARY

December 23rd

I woke up early today and looked at my diary. Only two more days to Christmas!

So, I got up, had breakfast and went Christmas shopping. Or rather, Christmas stopping. I kept stopping to think what to buy.

And then, changing my mind.

And then, changing it back again.

Oh, dear! I just cannot make up my mind. Ever!

For instance. I spent hours in the shoe shop deciding what to buy my best friend, little Miss Neat.

'I think I'll have those pink slippers with the blue bows,' I said to the salesgirl.

'Certainly, Madam,' replied the salesgirl and put them in a box.

'On the other hand,' I said, 'I think the blue slippers with the pink bows would be better.'

By the time the salesgirl had unwrapped the pink slippers with the blue bows for the fourth time and wrapped the blue slippers with the pink bows for the fifth time . . . I knew exactly what to buy.

So I went next door and bought Miss Neat a box of chocolates!

December 24th

Today is Christmas Eve.

Mr Muddle popped in to wish me Happy Birthday. He meant to wish me Happy Christmas, but that's Mr Muddle for you!

In the afternoon, I sat down and wrote a long letter to Father Christmas.

It was the longest letter I have ever written.

I just couldn't make up my mind what I wanted!

I used up ninety-nine sheets of writing paper trying to decide.

Ninety-nine!

Then, just before I went to bed, I thought of something else.

That made one hundred!

December 25th
Christmas Day!

I jumped out of bed and ran downstairs to see what Father Christmas had brought me.

There was just one large box, gift wrapped, with a note. It said, 'To little Miss Fickle, with love from Father Christmas.'

I unwrapped the paper, opened the box and peeped inside.

'Just what I wanted!' I laughed. 'One hundred sheets of best yellow writing paper.'

Then I stopped.

'On the other hand,' I thought . . . 'green would have been nice!

HAVE FUN!

Mr Tickle has hidden in the puzzle the names of the Mr Men and Little Misses that he's tickled today. Can you find them all? The names read across, or down, or diagonally. Circle them on the puzzle and cross them off the list below.

BOSSY BUMP CHATTERBOX FORGETFUL FUNNY FUSSY GIGGLES GREEDY HAPPY HELPFUL LAZY MEAN MUDDLE NAUGHTY NEAT PLUMP SILLY SMALL STRONG SUNSHINE

WHAT MISCHIEF!

Mr Mischief is planning some mischief! He's going to the zoo to let out one of the animals! Can you see which one?

IT'S MAGIC!

Here is a magic trick to try on your friends! It's a very wizardy sort of trick, so you will need a magic wand to wave when you say your magic words!

Making a magic wand

You can make a wand for yourself from stiff black paper or paper painted black. Roll the paper several times round a long thick knitting needle and glue down the edge. When the glue is dry, take out the needle. Then glue small strips of white paper round each end as shown. Hey, presto! You have a magic wand!

Multiplying magic

For this trick you need a thick hard-covered book and about 12 coloured counters. And your magic wand of course!

Take the book and show it to your friends. Ask one of them to choose a page and to put two counters on it. Close the book and place it on a table in front of you.

Explain that, with the help of your wand and some special magic, you will turn the two counters into many more.

Wave your wand over the book and say some magic words — Abracadabra does nicely! Now, pick up the book and gently shake it over an upturned hat or a bowl.

Everyone will be amazed to see a cascade of counters fall out!

How it's done

Get everything ready beforehand. Open your book at the middle and lay it down flat. You will see a gap between the cover and the pages down the spine.

Carefully push about ten counters into this space, then close the book. The counters will stay in position.

The secret

When you do the trick, make sure everyone sees there are only two counters on the page. Be careful to hold the book so that the hidden counters do not fall out! Close the book. Then do your magic! Shake out all the counters — the two your friend put in the book *and* the ones you hid in the spine!

It will look as if you have made the counters multiply!

LITTLE MISS SCATTERBRAIN GOES SHOPPING

Crack the code to discover what little Miss Scatterbrain wants to buy from the butcher!

THE CODE

A	B	C	D	E	F	G	H	I	J	K	L	M	N	O	P	Q	R	S	T	U	V	W	X	Y	Z
B	D	F	H	J	L	N	P	R	T	V	X	Z	Y	W	U	S	Q	O	M	K	I	G	E	C	A

THE CLUE

```
        B
  X  B  Q  N  J
  X  W  B  L
     W  L
  D  Q  J  B  H
```

THE ANSWER

```
        A
  L  A  R  G  E
  L  O  A  F
     O  F
  B  R  E  A  D
```

28

COLOUR!

Can you see Mr Messy? Only his eyes and mouth show! Colour his body a lovely, messy, scribbly pink.

SHADOWS

Which is Mr Funny's real shadow?

30

A SILLY JOKE

WHAT'S GREEN, LIVES IN A FIELD AND HAS FOUR MILLION LEGS?

ER...LET ME SEE NOW. GREEN, LIVES IN A FIELD AND HAS FOUR MILLION LEGS? I'M AFRAID I DON'T KNOW.

MR. NOSEY, WHAT'S GREEN LIVES IN A FIELD AND HAS FOUR MILLION LEGS?

SEARCH ME!

COME ON NOW, MR. IMPOSSIBLE, WHAT'S GREEN, LIVES IN A FIELD AND HAS FOUR MILLION LEGS?

FOUR MILLION LEGS? IMPOSSIBLE!

WELL, WHAT IS GREEN, LIVES IN A FIELD AND HAS FOUR MILLION LEGS?

GRASS.

GRASS?

SORRY.... I MADE A MISTAKE ABOUT THE LEGS!

A FUNNY DAY

One morning, Mr Funny woke up in his funny teapot house.

He made himself a funny breakfast. One cold porridge sandwich and a cup of cornflakes!

Then he went for a drive in his car, which, incidentally, was a shoe. Fancy that!

As Mr Funny drove along, the first person he saw was Mr Bump. He was bumping into things, as usual.

In fact, Mr Bump had been having so many little accidents that morning, he was looking very sorry for himself.

Do you know what Mr Funny did?

He stopped and pulled a funny face. Which made Mr Bump laugh. In fact, he laughed so much, he nearly laughed his bandages off!

Which made Mr Bump feel much better.

Mr Funny went on his way and, in a little while, he came across Mr Quiet, sitting all by himself.

And looking very sorry for himself.

'I've just met Mr Chatterbox,' said Mr Quiet. 'And he talked and talked and talked so much, he's given me a headache.'
Oh, dear!

So, Mr Funny got out of his shoe, quietly, and stood on his head, quietly, and pulled a funny face. In total silence.

Which made Mr Quiet laugh, quite a lot. Quietly, of course. To himself.

And after that, Mr Quiet felt much better.

Later that day, Mr Funny met a sad-looking policeman on traffic duty. He had been on duty all day and he was feeling very sorry for himself.

'Stop!' said the policeman.

He went inside and cooked a special supper for himself. Fried jelly and chips!

He was just settling down to watch his favourite television programme when the telephone rang.

'Smile!' said Mr Funny, as he pulled his funniest face ever.

Which cheered the policeman up so much, he nearly laughed his helmet off!

Then Mr Funny drove home to his funny teapot house.

'What a funny day!' he laughed.

It was little Miss Giggles. But was she giggling? She was not! She sounded very sorry for herself.

'I haven't giggled once today,' sighed little Miss Giggles on the telephone. 'I haven't found a single thing to giggle about, all day. I think I must be ILL!'

Mr Funny thought for a moment. Then he told her a joke. It was one of his best.

'How can you tell which end of a worm is which?' he asked.

Little Miss Giggles thought for a moment.

'I don't know,' she replied.

Mr Funny laughed.

'Just tickle him in the middle and see which end smiles!' he said.

Which made little Miss Giggles giggle and giggle and giggle until the tears rolled down her cheeks.

'I think,' said Mr Funny, 'you have been . . . CURED!'

MR.GREEDY'S FRUITY CROSSWORD

apple
banana
grape
lemon
peach
pear
plum
raspberry
strawberry

Mr Greedy is off to market to buy some fruit for his mid-morning snack! He has listed the fruit he wants but he has left out one of his favourites.

Can you fit the names of the fruit in the crossword, using the coloured letters that are already there to help you?

Now write the coloured letters on the line below:

E A O N R E

Unscramble these letters to discover the name of the fruit Mr Greedy has forgotten:

O R A N G E

THE SEE SAW

MR. HAPPY'S TEATIME TREAT

Here is a recipe for chocolate squares to serve when you have friends for tea.

CHOCOLATE SQUARES
You will need:
100g (4oz) plain chocolate
50g (2oz) butter or margarine
2 tablespoons golden syrup
150g (6oz) plain sweet biscuits (such as digestive or rich tea)

What to do:
1. Crush the biscuits into crumbs in a mixing bowl, using the end of a rolling pin.

2. Put the chocolate, broken into pieces, the butter and the syrup in a small pan. Heat gently until melted, stirring with a wooden spoon.

3. Add the melted mixture to the crushed biscuits and mix well.

4. Line a shallow 15cm (6 inch) square tin with foil. Press the biscuit mixture into the tin, smoothing the top with the back of a metal spoon.

5. Mark into 16 squares, put into the refrigerator and leave for about 1 hour until firm.

6. Cut into 16 squares, and serve.
   You must have a grown-up with you when you make this recipe.

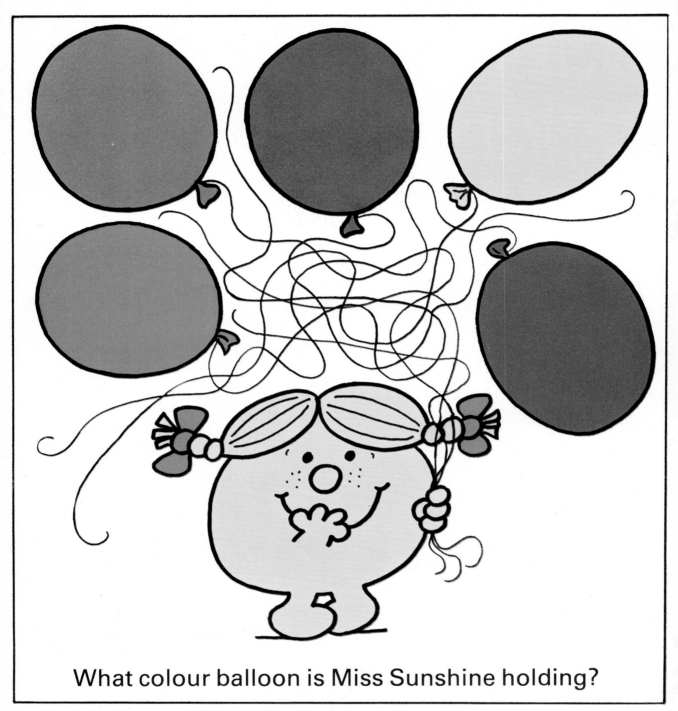

What colour balloon is Miss Sunshine holding?

44

A MATCHING PAIR

Mr Wrong wears shoes that do not match. One is brown and one is black. Can you help him find two shoes that make a matching pair? Write your answers below.

SHOES. B. AND. N. MAKE A PAIR

Can you rearrange the letters to help Mr Christmas deliver his parcels? They are all Mr Men names. Write your answers in the boxes below.

3. MR. C
ONU BE

1. MR. G
TSRNO

4. MR. G
OWRN

5. MR. S
IN KYN

6. MR. E S
ENEZS

2. MR. C M
ESFIH I

1	STRONG
2	MISCHIEF
3	BOUNCE

4	WRONG
5	SKINNY
6	SNEEZE

SPOT THE DIFFERENCES

Oh, dear! Little Miss Naughty has been in the library. Can you spot the ten books she has moved? When you have, colour the bottom picture.

47

MR. TICKLE IN TWOLAND

1. Did you know that there was such a thing as a tickle? Well, there is. Mr Tickle! He is small and round and has two extraordinary long arms. Which are very useful for . . . tickling!

2. One day, Mr Tickle decided to visit a funny sort of country called Twoland. Why Twoland? You'll find out soon enough! It was a long walk and on the way he passed some sheep.

3. Mr Tickle grinned and stretched out one of those very long arms. It reached right over the hedge and tickled one of the sheep in the field. The sheep nearly laughed its wool off!

4. Eventually, Mr Tickle arrived in Twoland. He caught a bus, a double decker, that took him all the way to Twotown. Then he walked down the High Street looking for someone to tickle.

5. There were two policemen standing outside Twotown Police Station. Mr Tickle grinned as he reached out to tickle them. 'Two tickles in one go!' he chuckled mischievously.

6. After that, he tickled two traffic wardens, two postmen and two waitresses in the Take-Away-Away restaurant. They were all doubled up laughing. Twice the tickles is twice the fun!

7. Then Mr Tickle met two little misses who looked very much alike. Little Miss Twin and Little Miss Twin. 'Hello hello,' they said. 'Hello hello,' replied Mr Tickle in Twoland double talk.

8. The twins invited Mr Tickle home for tea. When it was time to leave, Mr Tickle said, 'Just two more tickles before I go go.' 'Who for for?' they asked. 'Guess who who?' laughed Mr Tickle.

MR. DIZZY AND THE CLEVER PIG

DID YOU HEAR THE JOKE ABOUT THE CLEVER PIG WHO WANTED TO CROSS A RIVER?

NO.

WELL, THERE WAS A CLEVER PIG WHO LIVED IN A FIELD BY THE SIDE OF A RIVER. THE PIG WANTED TO CROSS THE RIVER BUT IT WAS TOO WIDE TO SWIM AND THERE WAS NO BRIDGE.

SO?

HE FOUND A BOAT.

TERRIFIC.

BUT THAT HAD A HOLE IN IT.

TOO BAD.

THEN HE TRIED TO FLY ACROSS BUT FELL FLAT ON HIS NOSE.

POOR CHAP!

NOW TELL ME, HOW DID THE CLEVER PIG GET ACROSS THE RIVER?

I GIVE UP.

SO DID THE CLEVER PIG!

STATION

Help Mr Slow find his way to the station.

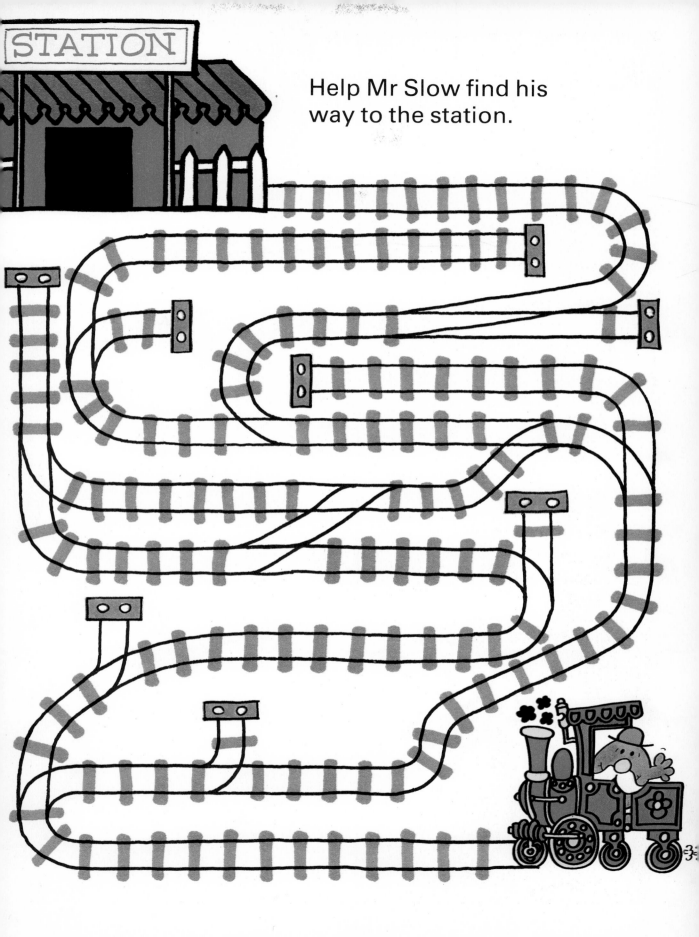

MR. SMALL'S NIGHT OUT

This story is all about Mr Small, who is probably the smallest person in the world. He lives in a tiny house at the bottom of Mr Robinson's garden. Underneath a daisy. That's how small he is!

One Christmas Eve, Mr Small had gone into town and had spent the day enjoying himself.

He had bought a Christmas present for Mr Robinson in the morning.

Then he had treated himself to an excellent lunch at his favourite restaurant. He had ordered a three-course lunch.

Two chips and a pea!

Which was quite a lunch for somebody as small as Mr Small.

54

In the afternoon, Mr Small had visited the library to change his library book.

Unfortunately, the book he wanted was on the top shelf. It took Mr Small all afternoon to climb up the steps to get it because he had to keep stopping for a rest.

And it was nearly closing time by the time he had climbed down again.

So you see how difficult some things were for Mr Small.

Then Mr Small had to run all the way to the bus stop to catch the last bus home. But the bus driver didn't see him and drove off without him.

Poor Mr Small!

He began to walk along the road. It was getting dark and it was beginning to snow.

Big, thick snowflakes fell from the sky.

Now, if you're as small as Mr Small, one snowflake is like a great big snowball landing on your head.

Thud!

So, you can imagine what it was like for Mr Small to be caught in a snowstorm, can't you?

Thud! Thud! Thud!

Mr Small did look miserable. It was getting late and Mr Small thought it would probably take him all night to walk home.

If not all the next day.

And the next.

He was beginning to wonder if he would ever get home, when suddenly he heard the sound of sleigh bells.

Mr Small looked up and there, flying towards him was, guess who?

Father Christmas!

'Hello,' said Father Christmas, bending down and picking Mr Small up out of the snow. 'You shouldn't be out on a night like this!'

'Hello,' said a very surprised Mr Small. 'How did you know I was here?'

Father Christmas winked.

'I know everything,' he smiled. 'Or rather,' he added, looking worried, 'everything, that is, except how to deliver this little parcel.'

'I am much too big to get into a mousehole,' said Father Christmas sadly.

'But I'm not!' laughed Mr Small. 'If you take me there. I'll deliver this parcel for you. Little Miss Tiny is a special little friend of mine.'

So, Father Christmas put Mr Small inside his fur pocket, which was a very warm and snug place to be, and flew off to Home Farm.

Father Christmas handed Mr Small a tiny parcel. It was addressed to:

Little Miss Tiny,
The Mousehole,
Home Farm.

Then, Mr Small crept into little Miss Tiny's mousehole and put the tiny parcel into her stocking. Then he crept out again.

The smallest Father Christmas in the world!

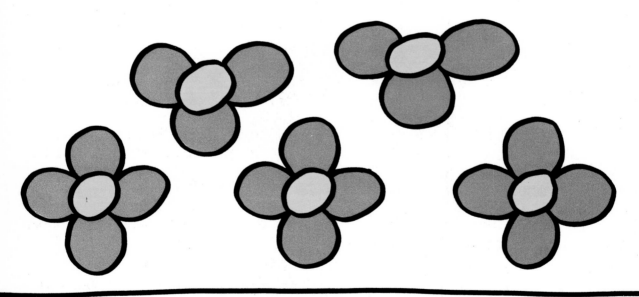

'Now, it's home for you,' said Father Christmas.

And he took Mr Small safely back to his tiny house, underneath a daisy, at the bottom of Mr Robinson's garden.

'I've got just one more present to deliver,' smiled Father Christmas, reaching into his sack.

'Who for?' asked Mr Small.

'You!' laughed Father Christmas, and handed Mr Small a parcel.

'But you mustn't open it until tomorrow morning,' he said. 'Goodbye now, and Happy Christmas!'

Mr Small was so excited, he hardly slept a wink that night.

Early the next morning, he sat up in bed and opened his present.

It was the perfect gift.

Something he had always wanted.

A special, fully automatic, thermostatically controlled, electric toaster.

Can you guess what was so special about it?

I'll tell you.

It toasted . . . one crumb at a time!